ACHAR DOSA

A Romantic Love Story

Ritesh Chandra Sahu
(Author)

Sunita Kumari Senapati
(Contributor & Editor)

ISBN: 9798719717784

This book has been edited and digitalised by E-sparX

https://esparx.in

PREFACE

With the changing time, we find that there are changes in emotions and feelings throughout the world. The book is a love story which casts love and all the harsh realities that poor people have to face in this superstitious world.

Any resemblance to any name, character, personalities, places, animals, etc. is purely fictitious and co-incidental.

My book is intended for entertainment of the young generation and I hope it will not be shunned by men and women. Great care has been taken into consideration, so as not to hurt the reader's sentiments.

- Ritesh Chandra Sahu

I am humbled and grateful to
Sunita Kumari Senapati,
whose ideas gave me proper direction
in bringing the sequence of
events in the story.
Her presence and effort has kept me
inspired in completing this story.

I would also like to thank
my parents for all the privileges that
they gave me and whose
contributions to my life cannot be
measured.

My Guide Map

"Sir, do you have an extra pillow?", asked Mrinal. I was too feeling cold, the bed sheet was thin, but what would he do with the extra pillow? I kept thinking in my mind, until the coach staff provided him the pillow.

He held it in his arms tight enough, as if it was something very expensive which he feared to lose. I was aware of the fact that thefts were common in long journey trains but he was a piece of mystery; a lot surprising. Few seconds later, he opened his eyes and gave a very auspicious look, making me feel like a thief, turned his back towards me and again held the pillow tightly, and embraced it.

"Ugghhh, it is pure nonsense", I murmured to myself.

My eyes were getting sore, I had been awake from the last 30 hours and my eyes required deep sleep". I turned my back, opened my specs, kept them aside and closed my eyes.

Sometimes, we wish we could do things, but we can't; our emotions are far more complicated then we think.

"O God, do bless this poor person. He is little creepy, but then, he was made so. His feelings and his emotions, all have left him in this unstable state. God bless you Mrinal." I prayed to God as I went to sleep and everything flashbacked in my mind that had kept me awoken the past 30 hours; he didn't let me sleep till his narration was complete.

"Bablu, I heard your father is throwing a party to his colleagues on his great business success."

"Yes, Mrinal and you know he has also invited many top level executives, politicians and business tycoons; and the district collector will be the chief guest."

"Oh Wow, aren't you going to invite us to this occasion?"

"Are you mad? Could I even celebrate in the absence of you all? And Mrinal, Guess what?"

"What?"

"You remember Anshu?"

"Who? Anshudhara Chingole?"

"I thought you had moved on in your life. But you remember her? She will also be joining the party."

"Disgusting, Why do you want to destroy the party by inviting her ?"

****

Anshu...Stupid, dumb and a crap...

Few years back

The train was leaving the station and I had to catch it somehow. My mom always bought small sized shoes. My pants had too become short, if it had been one inch shorter, I could be restricted from the school for wearing shorts instead of pants. I couldn't even run comfortably to catch the train. And, my bag was heavier than the paddy bags that I used to carry.

I frequently asked mom to change my uniform, but she always said that she will do it in the next season, when the fields will be greener and income will be higher.

This is the story of every farmer, who depends on the agriculture for their living. Finally, I got hold of the hand rail and I leapt high till my foot landed on the footboard and another landed on a shoe bigger than me.

"Awwwwwww". My hand, caught her hand, fair and soft; thin fingers, nail painted with tones of red. Her face was obstructed by the thin and straight black hairs. Her head had covered half of an ellipse before she could balance herself with her other leg.

She removed the hairs from her face and stared at me. From top to bottom... I was frightened, my body was shivering. I realized that I was crushing her foot. Suddenly, I removed my foot and also released her hand.

 "Sorry", I said as my head moved down. I was expecting a very bitter situation.

"Hahaahahaha, Are you a clown?", she asked.

A sense of relief, at least I was out of danger now. My mom always warned me to remain away from the girls, they can put you in danger anytime.

"You better tie a handkerchief before your pant. Everything that should have been inside, have come outside." She smiled with shyness as she said.

I looked down; the stitch of my pant had come out. "Oh shit!!! Mommmmmmm....", I yelled.

The beggar beside me who was begging pretending to be deaf and dumb, turned towards me and said "Pagal hai kya" (Are you mad)? The passengers started staring at me and then at the poor beggar. The helpless person quickly marched towards the other coach giving me a nasty look. Everybody laughed and it brought smile in my face.

For a moment, I forgot the disastrous incident that happened to me. But then the giggling of the girl had made me aware that I was not meant to come out from the shock so early. I removed my bag and hanged it in front of me. Although I was wearing my inners, it won't appear good.

"You look more like a clown than a student", She said with a cute smile on her face.

Her short lips, long nose and her triangular face, I hated it all and her black framed ugly glasses looked ridiculous.

Ashamed of the incident, I slowly walked towards the window seat and sat down, adjusting my bag over my lap, hiding the miserable state of my pant. Everything crossed past me as I sat motionless. I wanted the time to move very fast, so that I could reach home and sew up the pants.

I was deep inside my thoughts when a pleasant voice startled me.

"Hi!"

The girl sat in front me and offered me some fried nuts that she had brought from home. At first I denied, but then I couldn't resist my tongue, and I took two of them.

"Thank You", I said and she smiled.

The passengers stood up from the seat as the station approached. The girl adjusted herself nearer to the window, and she started crying. She looked towards me and held my hand.

"Please save me. They will kidnap me."

"What?"

"See they were seating comfortably and suddenly they have stood up. Do you have any sharp object to protect yourself, I have brought a jar filled up with chilli powder but it is now lost inside this whopping bag of mine."

"Okay don't fear, I am here", pretending to be hero of the story. "I will save you; till then, you search for the jar."

She opened the zip and completely ransacked her bag. In the mean time, I stared at every man; pretending to be protecting her from the suspect.

The train slowed down and the passengers got off the train. I burst into laughter.

"Are you travelling for the first time in the train?", I asked her controlling my smile.

"Yes, My dad used to drop me at the school by his car. But he is away for some business trip."

She didn't look beautiful, but her voice was very soothing.

"See, trains and buses all stop at some stoppages meant for public before reaching their final destinations, because you know they are public transport. "

Learning these, her eyes turned squeezed and her mouth wide open.

Nodding her head she said, "Ohhhh, and you were trying to make a fool of me?"

She slapped on my hand.

Who said that girl's hands are soft and their slaps don't hurt; I can say their slaps are enough to turn the epidermis red.

"I always went to the local school. My parents feared sending me to the city school."

"Oh, this is one thing I will also agree to. Your parents thought very correct." I giggled as I stated it.

"Do you think I am dumb and stupid?" and she kicked me and made faces. "My ammamma (granny) said that city people are bad, so I was a bit scared. Else, I am very brave and that is what I boast about myself."

This time I was controlling my anger. First she slapped me, now she kicked me; if my pants had been in good condition, even God couldn't have saved her from me.

Talks went by till we reached our destination. We got off and went on walking.

"Hello Miss, What should I call you?"

"My name is Anshudhara Chingole. In short, you can call me Anshu."

"So, Anshu...radha....Chag....lele..."

She interrupted, "Anshudhara Chingole; you better say Anshu"

"OK fine. So, you go to your class. I have some work nearby and then I will be going."

Frankly speaking, I didn't had any work, but the only reason of lying her was that I wanted to get rid of this crap. I talked with her only to prevent this lonely journey.

I was trying my best to maintain a safe distance from the girl. I had always learnt from my friends that, "GIRLS ARE VERY DANGEROUS FOR YOUR HEALTH. CLOSENESS WITH GIRLS KILLS."

"Oh, Now I know that you are hesitating to go to school because of your torn pant, right?"

"Umm..Hmm..Yes!" I didn't know from where she found out this, but it was a nice excuse to get rid of her.

"Okay, then you go but..."

"What but? Go now...", I screamed at the girl. She was disturbing my state of mind. I wanted to be alone. Not because I wanted to get rid of her, but because she reminded of my torn pants and now I was feeling bad. How will I go through the day, with a handkerchief tied on my pants and bag hung on my front.

"I am hungry", she said in a soft tone.

I could notice drops of water on her black shoes. The weather was not appropriate for rainfall, then what could it be? I turned upwards and downwards to glance at the sky and then her shoes, and it didn't take me time to realize that she was crying. I don't know why? But I felt very bad. My arms moved upwards towards her without having the control over my mind. I held her arm, and pulled her head towards my chest and gave her a light hug.

"Sorry Anshu. I didn't mean it. I was a bit upset about my situation."

She hugged me tightly, I felt like; like something that I couldn't understand but something very different happened. I felt as if the blood had stopped flowing in my veins, my breathe had stopped. But then remembering her dark specs and her face, I tried to loosen my arms, then removed her arms too.

"Okay Anshu. Did you ever eat the famous Achar Dosa.?"

 She moved a bit away and with her brows raised in question mark, "Achar Dosaaaa? Awkward name... No, never heard of it... Can we have it?"

I searched for some coins in my pocket. "five, one, two...Total- 8. And, and, and five in other pocket, and then 2 rupees in my pencil box with which I used to make circles in my drawing classes, and yes, Rupees 10 in my bag. So, eight, five, two and ten- a total of Rs. 25. And then minus six, for my return train journey. With this, I am left with Rs. 19 now. I needed Rs.1 more to get at least one Achar dosa."

"Anshu, I wanted to say... " I am very poor at telling lies, I have often been beaten up after saying lies.

So, I used to close my eyes or look towards other directions while lying.

"You know what? Here, the achar dosa is famous but recently I heard the veg upma is more tastier", I said calmly and in a very pleasant voice so as to convince her to take the second option.

Although I knew that the veg upma of that place was the most horrible upma with not a piece of vegetable to be found while eating. I remember that I always used to sit outside the stall near the groceries and gulping the upma thinking that the vegetables have been crushed and mixed with the upma. But, truly it filled my stomach. It was the cheapest food that I had in the city.

I waited for reply, "Anshu, are you again angry?" I turned towards her and then to my left and then to my right. I could feel the corner of my mouth forcing my lips to rise up and smile and yell. Yes, I was saved from that dumb girl.

"What the hell are you doing there, Arey, Oh Pagal *(Mad person)*?" The voice startled me.

"O God" I always feel that God has some personal problems from me, he takes revenge as soon as I start becoming happy. Anshu had already reached the stall and was peeking from the small wooden window and yelling at me.

I was lost in my thoughts. 'Will the shop owner beat me up, the tons of plates that I will have to wash, and then the groceries that I have to bring for him, and then serving foods and teas, and oh shit, my pants were also gone. I would better ask him for one towel or a lungi.'

"Will I send you a car to pick you? Can't you walk fast? See the poor old man had also crossed you." She shouted.

I increased my pace, walked up the stair.

As I reached the stall, my eyes fell upon the hotel owner – big dark eyes, the round moustache and such a fat belly... If this person comes to beat me for not paying the bill, I think his belly will collide and suffocate me before his sound reaches my ears. Every law of physics will fail, I will definitely get the noble prize for proving that fat belly is more faster than sound; but only if I will be alive till then.

I kept my bag on the chair and leaned to sit on the chair. "Bhai Ji, Achar dosa has been now priced to Rs."

"What?", my voice drew the attention of the customers. "Okay okay, no matter... Give us one.." I tried keeping myself calm, gave a big smile to all the customers- hiding my trouble inside me.

"But, madam has already ordered two of them."

I squinted at her; she was very happy and smiling. I wished Yamraj would come and save me from this situation. Now everything was gone. Everything was lost. The job of washing the plates was okay. At least no one will be seeing me. But, how will I reach my home? Everything was now in fast forward mode, Sweeping beneath the seats, acting like a disabled, singing and begging.. People watching me, saying "Aage badho Aage badho". "Sir, do rupay do na.", "Hatt, Bhhag yahan se."..... Oh God.."

"Dhadaam", I fell on the table; startled by the sound made by me, I looked at the customers. This was the second time the crowd stared towards me in an auspicious way.

"Sorry folks"

"Can't you sit properly.", I just nodded my head.

"Ye lijie Bhai ji apka Achar Dosa", said the waiter.

"Eat, eat all, Eat me as well", I murmered. "Bhookad". I was munching up the dosa having preoccupied with the stresses to guess the taste of the dosa.

"Yummy, Nice food... Arrgghhhhhhhh", She belched after eating half of the dosa. "Sorry, but I can't eat this anymore"

"Okay no problem, you can say this to the owner and he will charge you only for the portion that you have eaten", I said with my teeths closed. "Stupid"

"Sir, this is your bill. Only Rs. 50" said the waiter.

Rupees 50 and was it **ONLY**? 10 rupees more will make up my weekly train expenses. "Sir, Please bring me a tissue paper", requested Anshu.

What was this tissue again? She has eaten only half the dosa and now wants some other food. Hey bhagwan, save this little creature.

Keeping things aside, I started my business. This was the perfect timing for taking out and assembling all the coins. I was busy searching for coins, when the waiter again appeared before me with a box of tissue paper. Now what was it?

I quietly picked up one tissue paper thinking that he would even charge me for the tissues. I copied her actions, wiping the fingers and then the hands and then throwing the paper into the table dustbin.

I moved my hand in the bag pocket, grasped all the coins, "Sir, is there any vacancy here? You may need a person...."

I was interrupted by Anshu, "Sir, this is your 50 rupees." A crumbled note of Rs 50 taken out from her tiny teddy bear purse.

"Anshu, you need not pay it, I am paying it. It's Rupees 50 ONLY", I said it, but believe me I didn't mean it. From my whole senses I was praying God to not let her change her mind. It was only a FORMALITY.

"This time let me pay for you."

"Okay as you wish" I was extremely happy, joyous, glad, and so happy that words would fall short of.

I took one more tissue from the box that the waiter kept on the table. Taking the money the waiter went to the counter. I was sad that I could not enjoy the taste of the Achar Dosa. I had it only once when a friend of mine threw his birthday party.

"Anshu, You know, I don't like food to be wasted." Hoping she would clue of what I wanted, but she was dumber than I thought.

"But, I can't eat any more. This was too big for me to eat it alone."

"Okay no matter, I will eat it... " I leaned over the table, pulled her plate and started munching ."

She looked at me enjoying the Achar Dosa and gave a smirk look. I licked up the masala stuck to my fingers.

"Arrggghhhhhhh"- the sound of belch was audible to the diners there, but then I didn't care for it. It was an alarm that I was finally out of the one-hour heart stroking situation.

*****

Anshu really did save me from a big trouble and fulfilled my long lasting desire of eating the famous 'Achar Dosa'. I wanted to thank her a lot from the core of my heart, but I feared that it would give her a clue of my poor situation.

Wait, wait... Yes, I was praising her, but let me warn you, Please don't think that I started liking her. She was kind, but that doesn't mean that she was very good, and moreover, she paid my charge- my charge for tolerating her throughout the journey and helping her out with the breakfast. I was a mini broker, and she just paid the fees of a broker.

"Can I ask you a question?" Anshu asked slightly bending her head and looking towards my eyes.

"Do I have any other option rather than listening to your stupid questions?" I thought I would say her. But then my stomach was much full than expected and saying such a big line along with walking was more difficult than just accepting it. I nodded my head.

"You were searching for a job? For whom?"

O Shit..Half of my tongue came out before my teeth cut it. Hesitatingly I just blabbered, "Oh that job..that job... that job.. Yes I remember that job was for my uncle...He was looking for a job in the..."

"Say thank you", She cut my words before I could complete the lies. Did she guess that I had no money to pay for the dosa?

Hesitatingly I asked, "Thank You but why?"

She pointed towards a big poster. "SANAM TAILORS- since 1994"

"But what is a big deal in it, there are many shops here- BABA Tailors- since 1991, KUMAR TAILORS- since 2000, RAJA TAILORS- since 1998, and yes right behind the tree is another tailor, SUHANA tailors – since 1500.... Hahaha... I guess the Mughals used to make their turbans and dhotis from here..”

“Ohho...Chup (Quiet).” She screamed. “Let's get your pant sewed.”

Shock, again a bigger one. Out of the frying pan and into the fire. I had just recovered from the shock and again.... I felt I was moving, my legs went side by side. I guessed, I was overdosed with shock and going into traumatic situation. Control, control, control.. I pounded upon my chest to make my senses come alive. I turned my head back and the pea-brained girl was pulling me towards the shop. I had to say something to stop her.

“Anshu, my father is a tailor. I like when he sews for me. Please wait.’ I knew that my pot of lies was filling after meeting this creature but I was helpless.

"Okay but how will you manage with this torn pant. This handkerchief is meant to stay on your hands and not below your belly."

I was feeling a bit awkward. People stared at me as they crossed me, probably due to my odd appearance. I also wanted to correct up the pants but I had no idea of the price of sewing.

"Okay, how much will it cost?" I asked her. She repeated the same question to the tailor.

"Five rupees beti", came up the crooked reply from the old tailor. "Beta, take the towel from there and change the pants."

"Give me your bag, I will hold it", Anshu said softly. I was opening up the bag, but then something stroked into my mind and I denied. It would be a problem if she did find out the coins in my bags; it would be better if I keep my bag to myself.

Having changed my pants, I handed over it to the tailor. Anshu was smiling looking at my appearance, Shirt, beneath it a towel, on the shoulders a bag and on my foots, black boots with socks. I was looking like a modern street beggar.

The tailor looked at the pants, then, through the torn hole looked towards me and then towards the girl. "Beta how old is this pant?" He asked with a question mark in his face. "I have never seen so many stictches going criss crossed everywhere."

The tailor grinned and Anshu was covering her mouth with her palm; she turned her head to the opposite direction, controlling her smile. I was feeling very humiliated.

"No, actually it was gifted by my uncle- imported one. Don't you feel the difference in the cloth?" I said in a serious tone wanting to have a grip over the situation.

Now both of them burst into laughter. The tailor threw the pant on my face, commenting- "We don't sew imported pants, they are very delicate. You should better buy a new one or manage with the handkerchief. New one will cost you Rs. 100 for half pants and Rs. 150 for full pants"

I was ashamed of my situation. Anshu stepped towards me and with her heels up whispered into my ears, "I will pay for it, you need not worry. You can pay me later. And please take trousers this time; you don't look pretty cool with hairs on your thighs."

I denied because I knew my status. Morever, from the experience of my financial background I had learnt that it was impossible for me to repay this sum of money. But I also knew that my mom won't buy me a pant this year and I will have to manage it. I asked Anshu to come to a corner. I didn't want the tailor to get involved in our talks.

"Anshu, it's not about money. I have Rs. 500 in my bag but I like it when my father sews it up for me and my father is one of the prestigious tailor of my village." I walked towards the cloth rack while continuing my lies," I will........"

'Krrrriiiiiiiiinnnnnnnnnnnngggggggggggggg' echoed on the floor. I was confused as to laugh or to cry at my situation. All coins along with my 10 rupees note fell on the floor. The pocket of the bag was torn by a nail of the shelf. With no option left to keep my head high, my head automatically fell down with shame.

Anshu sat down as she counted, "one, two, five....and finally twenty five including the Rs. 10 note."

She rose up, lifted my palm up and handed me the coins, "Here, take your 500 rupees.... Hihihihi" as she giggled. I was going through my worst time. I just folded my hand full of coins and searched for my pant pocket to keep it, but remembered that the towel didn't have any of it.

"*Tāta* (*Grandfather*), please show a trouser for him of that color" Anshu said pointing towards the color of the college dress. The tailor handed it.

"Please try it and check the fitness" Anshu handed the pants to me. I had two reasons to cry, first- because I was humiliated in a very poor manner and second- because I was holding the trousers that I long had wished for.

I quickly went on to change my pants, handing over my bag and handful of coins to Anshu.

Having changed my uniform, I looked beneath and then towards Anshu, she smiled with her brows raised up and nodding her head with lips upwards- "Perfect, it suits on you".

I ran towards her and then hugged her tightly and shook her with happiness, "Thank you, thank you, thank you a lot".

But my raised happy lips moved down as I saw the tailor giving a angry look at me through the upper portion of his specs hanged not on ears but on nose, as if she was her daughter.

I removed my arms, took the bag from her hand and put the coins back into my pocket. She paid the money and I was just stepping down from the staircases, when the tailor shouted,

"Ae *chokra* (*boy- slang*), take this imported pant of yours and hang it in your prayer room and show *agarbattis* and *diyas* daily."

I turned back and ran from the shop hoping not to show him my face again.

*****

With time, things changed pretty fast. I had started ignoring her; though she used to call me to sit beside her, I sat on other seats far from her. I could see her staring at me, but I pretended to be unaware. I am not so bad, believe me, I didn't want to ignore her but I knew that I couldn't repay her debts, I had to collect the money and repay her. I tried to save money as much as I could.

Few days later,

I stepped out of the train. She came infront of me and blocked the pathway.

"Hi. Can I know the reason for your massive ignorance. Didi I do some mistake?", she had almost cried. Although I didn't see her, but her voice said everything.

I just denied replying saying 'Personal Problem'. I pushed her to the side and went on. I collected money for doing my friend's homework and by cutting down the expenses on my tiffins.I

n the tiffin breaks I would rush to the nearby field with my bottle full of water, sit on the field and complete my friend's home works for some money. I used the bottle of water to extinguish the fire of hunger. Within a fortnight, I had gathered Rs. 80. I required 70 more for repaying debts of pants and Rs.25 for the Achar dosa.

As the bell rang, the students rushed towards the canteen for the lunch. 'Today let's have pizza', 'I didn't have Samosa for many days', 'Half of the day over...', 'It's too hot here, why not have some drinks?', 'Hahahah', 'Oh yes, and then as he was about to eat the omelette, the.....'.

The sounds faded as the students went away from the class room. I sat with my head down. My stomach ached as if elephants rather than mice were jumping inside it. My mom couldn't prepare the breakfast due to her high fever. She asked me to take 15 rupees from the jar for breakfast and the ticket. I was already late for the train, so I just picked up some of the coins,put them into my pocket and rushed towards the station shooing the cows and the goats along my path.

As I reached the ticket counter to buy the tickets, I was utterly disappointed to find that all those coins that I had picked up were Rs. 1 and altogether they made only Rs. 7. Taking out the Rs. 2 coin from my pencil box, I bought the the up and down ticket, and was left with only Rs.1 now. I knew people have enemies, they too have enmity among the family members but my luck was my enemy, and it was such thing I couldn't even take revenge from.

Both of my hands squeezed my belly, it was unbearable. Tears rushed out from my eyes. I had also forgotten my coin bag in which I collected my money. I was left with no other option. The heavy amount of water inside my stomach was having tides, and it was asking for human bodies to gulp them into the deep ocean.

"Mrinal", came a voice very close to my ears.

I lifted my head up. For the first time, yes it was the first time that Anshu took my name. I can't describe the sound but my name from her mouth sounded completely unique, like the saffron and large cubes of sugar in the chocolate milk.

She opened her tiffin and kept it infront of me. While I was moving my hand to pick up a cake from the tiffin, she pulled my hands.

"First wipe up the streams flowing down from your eyes", Anshu said with a gentle smile in her face.

As I wiped my eyes, she picked up a cake, brought it towards my mouth and opened her mouth saying "Aaannn", indicating me to open my mouth. She put the cake inside my mouth.

I couldn't resist myself from looking at her, from looking at her face, from looking at her eyes, and her smile. She kept me feeding as I stared at her. She ate a piece of cake, and then fed me one; then again she would eat one, and then feed me the other piece...

"Hello Mrinal!", as she clicked her fingers in front of my eyes. "Stop munching, it has been five minutes since you took the last bite, there's not even a minute particle of cake in your mouth to chew." She gave me a smile full of shy, and went out of the classroom.

I was too deeply lost into my thoughts to realise anything. My stomach felt satisfied. And, I kept smiling myself remembering her face, though not very pretty, but then not even ugly. I cursed myself for hurting the girl so much and thinking so bad of her.

She came and sat beside me. "Are you well now?"

"Ya ya...." I paused for a bit. "Anshu, I am extremely sorry.... I shouldn't have treated you so badly"

"It's Okay Mrinal." She looked downwards as she said, remembering the bad time that I made her go through. I felt as if she was feeling bad for the treatment, but then with a smile again she lifted her face up and asked, "Is everything fine, Mrinal? I have been noticing for quite a few days that you are ignoring me. Is there any problem with me?"

I was very ashamed of my deeds. "Actually, sorry again. Please forgive me." I held her arms. "Please understand Anshu, I am not a thief. I will pay your money. I have been working hard enough for collecting money. I have saved half of the money and within 2 weeks I will be handing them to you"

"Mrinal, are you mad. I know your situation. I even know that you have been skipping your lunch to save money, but, had I ever asked you for it? Do you think that money matters more than you? I don't need the money. I want you Mrinal, I want you to be happy. I want you to be my friend. See, I am new to the college and I don't know anyone here, but only you; and you made me lonely these days."

I kept my fingers in front of her lips to stop her saying anything more, and then hugged her tightly. She was really a very good girl. She gave me a return hug. I heard the students coming and so we went to our seats.

From the day everything changed, we sat together, we ate together, we shared lots of gossips about the school, family life, aims in life, and much more. I was now free from doing home works of people and she taught me. We used to spend time very often, in the cafes and the malls. My father and mother had also opened a stationery shop and it was doing well. I used to run the shop after college and studied late night. Although the time was difficult, I had to struggle a lot, managing everything, but then I was happy, because then I didn't have to ask anyone for paying the money. I could afford my necessities and also could feed Anshu sometimes.

*****

Someone very truly stated, "Time flies like the wind, when you are happy; and stops by when you are in a bad mood."

Since the time we became friends, I smiled more, I remained happy and my business grew profitable. My studies were going well and most important was the smile on my parents face which had returned after decades. My teachers and professors who used to hate me, had recognised me for my hard work that I did. She was indeed a turning point of my life. The changes within me and around me in these past 5 years was quite significant, and not to forget, it was all because of Anshu.

*****

It was the last day of our school before the examination. Our school was not affiliated, so we all had different centres for examination. And it was the final meet with everybody. The teachers and our juniors had organized a farewell party for us. Everyone had big smiles on their face, but then, within those smiles also laid the immense grieves of breaking the bonds that we had during these times.

I knew that the friendships, jokes, fights, hidden loves; quarrelling, arguing, attacking upon other's tiffins, pulling legs, backstabbing friends, and all will be gone. The only things that will remain with us for the life time are the memories; in which every enemy shall be a friend, no matter how worse they treated us.

"Mrinal, why not join us and where is Anshu?" asked Balbir, a friend of mine. They were cutting cake, and everybody was present there, except her. I went out and searched for her everywhere, from the classes to the field, from the canteen to the waiting room. As I was crossing the hall, Pushpa came and said that Anshu had locked herself inside the washroom and was not opening the door or responding.

I was frightened and I ran towards the ladies washroom. I banged the door. "Anshu.....Anshu...", I shouted but there was no response from the other end. I was horrified and couldn't understand what to do.

After sometime I heard the sound of the door latch as it cranked and with a big swing she opened the door, and pulled me inside. The adrenaline rushed into my blood and my eyes and mouth went wide open with surprise. She took me in her arms and hugged me tightly as if we were meeting after decades. But, more than the surprise, I was scared, not because she had held me so tightly, but because I was inside the ladies washroom. Pushpa who was stressfully standing at the door, now smiled and turned away her head with shyness.

Anshu kept sobbing, "Mrinal, when will you meet me again? It was very nice being with you, and I don't know why time passed so quickly. Wish schools had never ended. Reply me Mrinal, reply me....." Her voice tore as she said.

I held her arms and wiped her tears. "Arey, I am with you always. Let's go and enjoy the farewell, you know this is the last time when we will all be present together. Everybody is waiting for both of you. Come soon and attend the cake cutting ceremony."

She smiled and then again hugged me, "After the farewell, please wait a bit. I have something to give you."

*****

The cake cutting finished. The principal of the school gave the speech and some refreshment programs were arranged for us. One by one everybody was awarded gift packages, and then after the food distribution, we hugged each other and shook hands with the teachers before waving them a final bye, 'a Good Bye'.

I waited for Anshu, outside the premises. She held my hands and pulled me. We walked side by side but there was a difference- "SILENCE". Silence followed us. Neither did I say anything, nor did she say. We just moved on and on till we reached the food stall where we first ate "Achar Dosa", ordered two of them. Recalling the things about the first day that we met, she said everything, about how she felt with me, and how she was frightened, my torn pants, how I shouted at her and she cried, how I munched upon her leftover Achar Dosa and how the tailor made fun of me.

The girl whom I had always seen making fun of me and joking about, seemed a bit odd that day.

Though she laughed at some points but it didn't take time for her face to change expressions.

As she talked, she kept feeding me half of her dosa, and talks went on.

"You know Mrinal, I will miss you very much."

"I will also miss you, Anshu"

"I don't know whether you know or not; you are far different from other boys and I thank God for bringing you to me. I wish the school had continued and it had not ended."

I continued to listen at her while eating the dosa from her hands. "You are really such a nice guy, and you know what? Being with you, I never felt odd or creepy. I could be as much frank with you as I wanted. I could say you anything, treat you on my wish, and you would listen to my *bakbaks* without even interrupting me. We studied together, ate together and made jokes together."

Their was an unusual softness in her tone.

"I feel very comfortable with you. And I think I like you, not really like you.. But I LOVE YOU."

*****

"Mrinal, leave me. Mrinal leavve me or else I shall kill you, go from here. Ahhh Mrinal please leave me, I am suffocating. Mrinal". Describing about his past, Mrinal had got hold of me. He held me tightly in his arms. The passengers from the nearer berths had all gathered to listen to his story.

It was not only me who had been awake since the past 30 hours, but they had too contributed their time. Many, got off the trains when they reached their destination and many newcomers made themselves comfortable near us.

Usually, I used to go by flights in economy classes, but the flight was cancelled due to heavy flood in the airport. It was the first time that I had decided to go by train.

About 30 hours before

I had made myself comfortable in the AC compartment, when I noticed that a passenger infront of me was not very comfortable. At times, he looked outside the foggy glasses and then after every five minutes or so, he laid his legs out to sleep. I saw him repeat these actions many times.

Out of curiousity, I asked him, "Is everything Ok? Are you having any problem?"

At first he denied to answer and turned his back, but then, he woke me up and narrated the whole incident that happened with him.

Hearing me yell at him, he realised that he was squeezing me.

"Ahhhh, sorry, I was lost into her thoughts."

As he loosened his arms, I tried to regain my breathe.

Mrinal said, "This is the first time that I am traveeling in this AC compartent of the train. I never knew that trains have different compartments and they also have food for free."

He grabbed the evening snacks that was provided my the caterer.

"Nothing is free. All these pricings are added up in the train fare.", I murmured as I chewed the sandwich.

"Ohhh!! Actually I have no knowledge of it. Bablu's father had booked a ticket for me to invite some of his colleagues."

"Okay. So, did you go alone?"

"Yes. Bablu had dysentry and his father was busy in his meetings. So, I decided to go and invite them. They are sitting in some '2A' compartment and I am sitting here."

I remembered that we had deviated from the topic. I, as well as the passengers were eagerly waiting t listen the story.

"Let's continue. What happened next. She said that she loves you? Did you too reply back to her? You must be happy then? What is the thing that has burdened your heart?"

Mrinal asked for the time.

"9:30PM."

The train was much delayed. An eight hour journey had already taken 30 hours and there was more to go, but hope we would cross the flooded region soon, and then everything would be fine.

Mrinal said, "Can you check the approx time to reach my destination."

"Okay", opening the application, I typed in the location as he spelled.

"40 minutes more.."

"Ok fine. I am feeling a bit unwell. This is the first time I am having such a long-time jouney. And the story is not as you expect. 'Love is not so easy journey in a developing society.' In brief, we were separated. But, Anshu is coming again to Bablu's function, and this time I have thought of that I will be making everything clear. Won't it be better, if I will say the story after reaching a climax?"

Everyone denied. They wanted to listen to the exact details that had happened. I was also among that. It was a kind of suspense.

When the passengers were tired of requesting, all of them went to their berths making faces at him. Mrinal asked the coach for the pillow, held it in his arms and then stared at me.

"Please wake me up at the station."

"Ok", I knew that somewhere in his heart, he was having a very deep emotion of love and heart break. Either he is unable to understand it, or he doesn't want to understand it.

Few moments later

The train honked.

"Hello Mrinal. Wake up, your station has arrived."

He woke up, got hold of his small cloth bag. His appearance was a bit odd, his dresses and the AC compartment didn't fall in a line.

"Hello Mrinal, How would I contact you incase your story is complete?"

He smiled and said, "I don't have any mobile. I don't have emails too. If the destiny arranges a meeting, I shall say you everything."

"Ok wait." I searched for paper in my pockets, but it was not there. Finally, I got a Rs. 50 note and wrote my mobile number and email on it. "Take this, if someday if you feel that your story has an ending feel free to contact me."

"Okay", he took it, smiled and left.

*****

Years went by and I had almost forgotten him. I had never expected that he would call me, but one such evening, an unknown number ringed my mobile.

"Hello"

"Hello, do you remember me?", heard from the other end.

"Sorry, but may I know your name?"

"Mrinal"

The name seemed heard of, but I couldn't remember. While I pressurized my mind to remember it, he said, "Do you remember the train journey... heart broken story... Achar Dosa and the girl....?"

"Oh yes, Mrinal. Now I could remember everything. Have you reached your conclusion?"

"I believe so", said he in a slow tone.

"So, did she come to you? Was it a happy ending or a sad one?"

"Could we meet please?", requested Mrinal.

We decided the time and the location.

*****

I was waiting in the office. He knocked the door and entered.

"Welcome Mrinal, sit here"

His hairs and beard looked even worse. May be he had a very bad time. His dresses were muddy and his shirt hanged loose.

It made me no time to realize that he had become mad. May be Anshu had left him forever, and he has turned depressed.

He sat down and sipping the cold drink, he continued.

When Bablu reminded me of Anshu and said that she will be coming, I felt a bit upset. I wanted to ignore her. Tears ran down from my eyes reminding of all those times spent with her and as I stood with Bablu. I just held his hands.

Bablu said, "It was my entire mistake to say you about Anshu. You have not met her till now and have made me senseless; what would happen, when you will meet her? Mrinal, with folded hands I request you to kindly control your feelings, because there will be bigger personalities in the occasion. And yes, please don't hook yourself up"

I only smiled and winked at him...

"Now stop behaving like a girl and let's go home. I don't know where to start from. A great deal of task is left to be organised. Go and have dinner and directly go to your bed and sleep as early as you can, tomorrow we will have to arrange everything up and remember you have to wake up early", Bablu said me commandingly.

Bablu was a great friend of mine; he brought me back from the mess and controlled me. Although he was younger than me, but I was proud of the man, he was a real man by heart by soul. Getting a friend like this in these days was nothing less than a Great Luck.

That day, after I got down from the train, Bablu received me. Days went by we did arrangements for the meeting.

*****

Chapter 6: A difficult but good decision

That day as Anshu proposed me in an unusual way. I really felt nice, but I knew that things weren't as much easy as I thought.

'Although I liked her, but I didn't love her. There were many differences that arised in my mind. She used to spend luxuriously but my family depended upon agricuture. The money that we earned from the stationery and the harvest was sufficient only to feed our stomach and keep something for future. I knew that I could never afford her anything.

Her caste was higher and I was just of a low caste. How could I make my parents agree for all these? I can't even think of passing time with her, because I knew her- I knew how emotional she was, and I couldn't hurt her.

Moreover, there was nothing that could keep us together. I knew it well that this was the last that I met her and she met me.

I couldn't just force my parents for a mobile phone. My parents couldn't afford a trouser for me, could they bring me a mobile and that too, for chatting, and all those call expenses…. Our paths, aims, goals and life, all will be forked in a few moments from then.'

I had to do something to make her realize that I was not fit for her. Although it took a great courage to speak something, but I had made my mind.

"Hello, Anshu…", I shouted, "What are you saying? Go away from here… I never thought you would do this? Go and look at your face, go and look at your specs. Who will like to love you? I would never. You stupid creature, you don't match my status. Take your money…"

Saying this, I handed her Rs. 500 that I had deposited in these years.

Yes, I felt bad while saying all these, but I knew that I had broken her up completely. She would now have no feeling left for me.

A single dose of heavy insult is much better than continued doses of small insults. Therefore, I continued insulting her, till she went away, throwing the money on my face.

"You think that buying me a Achar dosa would make me love you.. Hell No….", I shouted as she went crying and running…

Seeing her go away from near me, my legs trembled and I sat down.

Anshu's heart was broken, and on the other hand I was broken, completely, for the sake of her future and for my parents happiness.

My days were spent in the fields, nights in the shop till the college opened. I remained away from the girls of the college, and they too didn't care because I looked different from them. I studied hard and got three placements from top MNCs, but didn't join any of them; my parents denied to leave their agriculture, so I had no other option than to live with them. At their old age, how could the son go and enjoy the millionaire life while leaving their old parents working in fields?

Bablu and I became friends and we spent the days casually, sitting in groups and roaming in the nearby villages, teasing and playin with small children.

My father sent me to work in nearby places, but my ego and my qualifications didn't let me allow to do these mini jobs.

The night was cold and millions of twinkling star-like bulbs added to its beauty. All arrangements had been done well by me and my friends. The stage was decorated with white color scented jasmine flowers with a dark blue background on the back. About 500 seats were arranged on the open field. I had been too busy since past few days, because it was all my responsibility- a responsibility given to me by my friend and I couldn't hurt his sentiments.

The function was about to begin in a few hours and I was busy discussing the sequence of events. I had to check everything- starting from the stage microphone, to speakers and food and seating arrangements. Bablu had helped me in everything, and this was a good time to repay some of the debts of friendship. Generally, Rich friends are so busy with other rich friends that they seldom look upon the poors, but Bablu didn't even let me realize my status. I was feeling happy that I was doing something for him and his family.

A black color, convertible open air Audi stopped past me, followed by two other cars. Two bodyguards with heavy arms got out of the car and opened the rear door. Mr. Rajhans (Bablu's father), the great personality of the day stepped out of the car; from the other side came out Bablu. Mr. Rajhans looked at me and smiled, perhaps he was impressed by my decoration. I smiled back and got back to work.

Bablu was busy welcoming the guests, while I was busy serving the drinks to the guests.

Actually, serving drinks was an excuse. I was searching for someone. My eyes were busy hunting for the girl who didn't seem much beautiful by her face, who was dumb; but who is now beautiful and who is not dumb.

"She was not sitting in the first row, nor was she in the second row, nor in the third, fourth, fifth, sixth, seventh and not also in the last row.", my heart and mind kept discussing, while my eyes were truly expecting to see someone.

Tired by my hunting eyes and my physical strength, I made myself comfortable on the last seat that was empty.

"Such an idiot, has he come here to sleep?", came a sound from the crowd.

I was too tired to respond to anyone.

"Yes, I was saved from this inhuman creature", came another voice. But this voice was somewhat known... Who might be it? Anshu? Was it she?

I shook myself up on the chair and opened my tired eyes just to look at her once. I remember her voice, and yes, I swear, it was her voice. But where is she?

I looked at the crowd of girls sitting in the sixth row and making fun of me, but she was not found, until one of her friends took her name.

"What? Impossible".. She couldn't be so beautiful, she couldn't look so pretty, she couldn't be Anshu. To make sure if she was Anshu, I moved a bit closer moving my steps forward slowly and slowly with fear in my eyes and curiosity in my mind.

I stood behind her.

She was looking towards the stage. I called her slowly making sure that other members wont get disturbed.

She looked back, gave me a grim look and then again turned towards the front. My heart pounded faster.

"Anshu", I called her again.

It did not even bother her. Was she ignoring me? No, I have to first check her if she is the same girl or is someone look-alike with a matching face? May be I was just day dreaming.

'Uh ho, who cares? I am just too tired, I must take a nap.'

Finding a vacant chair, I made myself comfortable. "Hello, Ms. Anshudhara Chingole." I jumped up from my seat. "Congratulations on your promotion to the business leader." The old man moved his hand forward.

The beauty stood up in front of my eyes. She shook hands with the man, with a smirk smile on her glowing face, she replied, "Thank You, sir. That's all due to your blessings."

'Business Leader? Unbelievable, she was a dull-witted personality.'

I was now sure that she was the same Anshu. But why did she ignore me? Perhaps due to my grown beard.

Rushing towards the home and then directly towards the bathroom, I got hold of the razor; sprinkled water on my face, heavily foamed up my 3 years old perfectly V-shaped beard, and then in 9 mixed strokes horizontally, laterally and vertically, it was all gone. 'Perfect shave'. I looked at my dresses, all had become dusty and my body... ewww... It was giving a pungent smell.

Rotating the knob to full flow, I showered myself, shampooed my hairs, wiped my body up and was ready with my navy blue blazers.

As I tramped out of my room, my parents stared at me astounded. I smiled at them, and then rushed quickly to save myself from the rapid fire quiz round from my parents. This new set of royal blazer was gifted to my father by one of his friends; I knew he would be angry, but I couldn't miss my chance on Anshu.

It was the first time that I was wearing this heavy suit. It was a bit uncomfortable, but I adjusted myself.

"Hi Anshu", I just moved my hand forward to shake, "How are you? And yes, congrats on becoming the project leader."

"Sorry, I didn't recognise you. And who is this Anshu? My name is Ms. Anshudhara Chingole, Ms. Anshudhara Chingole. I think that you have some confusion."

"Anshu, don't you remember me, I am Mrinaaa….."

She flashed her palm and sat down and then again stood up. She grumbled, "Whatever your name is, I don't think I have ever met you. You must clear your mind and your confusion. And let me remind you again… that, my name is Anshudhara Chingole and not Anshu."

I felt ashamed and insulted in front of her friends and some unknown guests. Turning back, I was just about to go. "And you, stop there. Shaving your beards won't make any magic. You look like a featherless chicken inside a black bag popping out its head. Those dusty smelling dresses suits you more than this classic uniform."

Who said boys don't cry? Boys cry, when they are sad. But the only thing is that, they can't show their tears to anyone, as it represents their weakness.

I went back to my house, put my mobile in flight mode, removed the blazer and with my shorts on, put the AC in the coolest mode, covered myself with blanket and cried. This was the first time that I was insulted so badly, I felt very offended, guilty and angry upon myself.

*****

⍰

Near Bablu's home

"Mrinal, you didn't attend the function?"

"Accctuuuuaaaaalllyyyyyyyy…."

"Yes, your mother said that you had a severe headache", said Bablu.

"Ohhh… I remember…. Actually, I had thought the drinks were just sodas, but it came out to be wine, and I drank a full glass of it without even knowing."

He laughed, "Perhaps you had the experience. It's good."

I didn't reply.

"Anshudhara was looking so gorgeous in her business outfit. Wasn't she?"

My friend had just picked the topic which my mind was searching for.

"Yes, I heard that she had been promoted to some leader."

"Project, Project leader. She is a tycoon in her field – an intelligent, beautiful, dynamic, cool and passionate person. You know, from the gossips, I also learnt that she would be handling a mega international IT project, and if she achieves success in it, she would be made the ambassador of the International Innovative Technology Conference."

"I had attended many such conferences before. It doesn't matter me, I hate those conferences...public talks... Lots of crowds with no intention and interest..."

"Great leaders always say, think twice before speaking. This conference is not your school conference or a general public meeting conference. It is the World's biggest conference and for the first time, in these 11 years, our country has been nominated for this conference. You dumbass, you won't know all these."

I felt too stupid. The previous day, Anshu insulted me and that day, my own friend called me a dumbass. May be, he is correct, I don't have a job and I have to depend on my old parent's hard work. It is so sad.

"With all these college degrees and lots of big certificates,

A person needs small papers that have values.

And in this world, anything that counts are only these small papers

And not collection of big certificates"

I just gave him a small smile, "Okay Bablu, I will meet you later. I have some work in my home." I went away with a heavy heart. My friends made me realize in 2 days which I couldn't realize in the past 4 years –' the value of money and position'.

My legs trembled as I walked. My world had shaken apart; I was going through a very worse situation of my life and who knew that the worst was waiting for me at my home.

*****

Somehow, I reached my home and rested myself on the old cranky bed. Lifting my legs up, I just bent down to lie, when 3-4 peasants shouted at the door.

"Mrunu betaaaa..", shouted a panting old woman.

I jerked myself up from the bed. "Beta, your mother had fallen unconscious in the field. She is having some problem. Your father and some of other farmers had taken her to the government hospital."

I couldn't wait to listen to them; my adrenaline rushed; Getting hold of my neighbour's cycle, I paddled as hard as I could, taking every shortcut, through the fields.

My father was waiting at the road side. "Beta, beta..."

"Papa.... Is everything right? What happened to Maa?"

"Beta, the doctor said that something in her heart has stopped and they need to urgently shift her to the City Hospital. There is no ambulance available right now. I fear something might happen."

I was unable to control myself. My eyes were turning black, but I had to control the situation. I knew that only I could handle my father.

"Your Rabin uncle has gone to bring his cart then we will take her to the city hospital. This government hospital is also not allowing her inside."

Such a poor administration. Hospitals, which are meant to look after the health of the people are denying for saving one's life?

'Oh God, thank you for this grace of yours. When you see the helpless, you deny help; when you see the happy ones, you give them everything.'

"Papa, bring Mom here."

I took my cycle near her, where she laid holding her chest.

"Papa, Rabin uncle might be late, and with the cart we will be even more delayed. Better, I would take her to the hospital."

I sat on my cycle, and my father tied her to the cycle and with my body with a few towels that we could gather.

I just looked at Maa and said, "Mom just take deep breathes and hold me tightly."

Without even a minute pause, I paddled, as fast as I could. Metres and kilometres went by. Hundreds of vehicle riders noticed us, but no one helped. I couldn't see anything, understand anything or think anything. Just my eyes focused on the roads, the shortcuts and the ditches. My legs were not worried, nor tensed and not paining. Only thing that I could feel was that I was gasping to breathe.

Up through the "ONLY FOR AMBULANCES. PRIVATE VEHICLES PROHIBITED" ramp, 90 degree turns and crossing some benches, directly I braked near to the ICU, shouting out the whole distance, "Doctor Saheb, doctor sahib". I had remembered the path because I used to take Bablu's mother to the ICU when she fell ill. Bablu used to be busy with his friends and her father busy in his work. Being a useless jobless and family dependent guy, I had to do all these.

The guards, who had rushed throughout the hospital behind me for breaking the rules of the hospital had all stopped, looking at my Mom's condition. The attendants dragged the stretcher, un-winded the towels, laid my mom and directly took her to the ICU. A security in-charge said something on the walkie-talkie and the doctor rushed in to the ICU, and then the sisters went in and went out.

I had also fallen apart, my body went beyond my control and I lost my senses, "Dhadaammmm". I could only realize what was happening but was not in a state to do anything.

Someone held my hands and someone my legs, and then I was laid down on some bed, perhaps a stretcher, and then what happened was unknown to me, until I woke up.

*****

When I opened my eyes slowly, I could see my father standing near me and holding my hands. Tears streamed down his eyes. Seeing me regain my consciousness, he wiped his tears by dragging the towel off his shoulders.

Raising my body with a jerk, "Papa, How is Maa now?"

He kept himself in the mute mode and then started crying again. Then he began with an intermittent tone.

"Doctor says, your mother, your mother.."

"Dad, what has happened please say?"

"Your mother needs urgent surgery within a week. Or else, she will…"

"Papa, then what are you waiting for? Go and ask the doc to start the surgery"

"Beta, we don't have enough money to have the surgery done."

"Papa, I have Rs.100 in my pocket and we also have money in the earthern piggy bank. Why not use it now?"

My mother used to put some monthly savings in a mango shaped piggy bank. She always used to say that with this money she would buy a gold necklace for my wife.

"Beta, you are very innocent; how will I make you understand? That much money is not enough."

"Then, how much?"

" One lakh…."

"Whatttt? One laaakkkkhh?"

I was awestruck. That was a huge amount. I remembered the day when I used to calculate the coins and used to eat 'Achar dosa', and today, these coins have no value when kept near this total sum of money. 'One Lakh'.

God was so egotistical with me. First the humiliating incident, then my gone beard, then my mother's sudden problem and then one lakh...

'Why God? Is this all because I am poor?"

"Papa, why not ask for some help to Bablu? His father is a great businessman, he will surely help us."

"I have left no stone unturned. He just made some excuses. Big people always have bigger responsibilities, and we are just... ", he paused, "We have no other hope, except selling our agricultural land."

"Papa, but it is our only source of income... What will we do after that?"

"Your Mom's life is more important. If necessary, I will beg and will feed both of you."

Hearing these words from the mouth of an old father, I couldn't keep my head high. I felt ashamed of myself. My father had spent his entire life in the fields, eating just stale rotis (chapatis) for teaching me; and here, I, having completed my education, do nothing but roam in the village.

I couldn't resist myself, pulling the glucose needle from my hand; I cycled again towards my home. Stuffing all my dresses into an old torn tote bag, I paddled again through the fields. My emotions were not under my control.

My eyes, my mind could only see and think of only one thing – my mother.

Showing my visiting card, I just ran towards the ICU and hugged my father.

"Papa, bless me. For the first time, I am doing something. I am going for some interview." I did not know where to go, how to go. "Just say Mohan uncle that I will return his bicycle in a few days. Till then just find a land dealer and get the loan, and start the operation. I have asked Bablu to sign the documents before operation. "

I touched my father's feet. He got hold off my shoulders, and kissed on my forehead.

"I am happy to have you as my son. Beta, take care and return soon. I will wait for you."

I just turned back to go, when my father shouted, "Beta, take the blazers for the interview..."

I remembered Anshu's comment on me and my blazer. 'Chicken without feathers popping his head out of the black bag'

"No Papa, it's okay.."

I rushed and paddled. My legs went on.

*****

"THE JOURNEY WAS
UNKNOWN, THE
DESTINATION WAS
BLURRED."

"Is there any job that you know? Are there any vacancies somewhere nearby? I have completed my MCA." I approached every man that came my way. Some denied, some just ignored and a few gave a very awkward look.

"Need a delivery boy…", came a sound from some distant.

I turned my head towards the right and then towards left. I found a big fat man with long moustache waving his hands.

'A delivery boy? But it won't pay much even to earn 2000 this month. How would I arrange 1 lakh? ', I thought in my mind. He came near me.

I hesitated but then directly approached him, "What will be my salary? Actually I urgently need money within a…". He didn't even let me complete my words.

"Rs. 1000 per night."

"One thousaanddd??????", I asked in surprise.

"Yes but the condition is that you will have to work only during night and keep this business as secret."

"What is this business about?"

"Second condition is that you will never ask about the business. Remember your job is delivering the items to the customers, and if you try to be over smart, your job will be gone."

I just nodded. Money was my need, I knew it well. 1000 per night would make 7000 this week.

"Okay so meet you tonight, correct at 10 PM. I will say you the third condition when you reach here tonight", he said with his heavy voice.

Things were not Okay, nor was I. I was too tired and hungry.

"Hello, Sir. I would work, but I want to request you something?"

He gave me a very stern look. "I need something to eat. 2000 plus my dinner please?", my eyebrows moved down, eyes shrinked as I requested.

He kept staring at me from top to bottom for a minute before agreeing. Tired and impatient, I waited for my food to arrive.

*****

My body ached after waking from a small nap after the heavy meal. The sun was shining on my head, perhaps it was noon. There was much time left to 10 PM.

A job in the day time would be much better.

I washed my hands and face, splashed some cold well water on my head. I felt a bit refreshed from the scorching sun. My legs started paddling again.

I stood near a big building, somewhat about 10 storeys with glasses all around. It reflected the rays of sun on my face. Boys, Girls, Women, Men – some went in and some went out. There were long queues outside. A poster above me read, "Vacancies Open"

Having parked my cycle, I walked forward until the security stopped me.

"Hello Mister, you need to register your name here before entering. It is lunch time now, come later."

It was better to wait then to come back later.

I registered myself with my lengthy dragged cursive writing. The guard stopped me again and turned the register towards him, snatched the pen from my hand and then wrote as I dictated.

The big sliding door opened after a while. The queue went in slowly one by one. People came out, but no one seemed to be happy. I tapped the shoulder of the person standing in front of me; he turned back, looked at my dresses and then took his tongue out, "Chii", turned to the front and stepped forward away from me.

I felt uncomfortable. There were so many people; everyone was well dressed with nice shoes, but I?

No one was behind me. I was the last candidate waiting for the job; a job whose details were too unknown to me.

Time went by and my heart thumped faster than usual.

I spoke to myself, "Do you deserve this job? You are not even well dressed? You are shameless, ridiculous."

My head hanged down with shame but I had no other option. The time on the big wall clock in front of me showed 4 PM.

I knew the interviewers would laugh at me but I didn't care, because, at that moment, they were not alone, the whole world laughing at my situation; And I could bear my insult, because my mother was waiting for me, she was fighting between her life and her death.

The gate opened and I went in. I was ready; ready to be laughed at. But I was not disappointed. I was just myself, unlike others, I didn't show off. If being a poor was my mistake then being rich was their mistake too.

As I entered, my hands and feet trembled. I was nervous, not because of my dresses but because I was standing in front of a big bench of interviewing members. The name plates read, "Mr. Bipin Arora, HOD, IT", "Mr. Nandkumar D'souza, IT CS", "Ram Lakhan Yadaw, Sr Mgr

HRM", "Jayas Choudhary, Mgr Special Services", "Shivam Kumar Agrawal, Project Assistant", "Anshudhara Chingole, Project Manager."

What? What was it that I just read?

"Anshudhara Chingole..", the racing beat of my heart pulsated even faster.

I was now convinced that my 1% chances of getting the job had gone down to 0% 'NULL'. I closed my eyes, took a deep breath and was about to leave, but something stopped me. My situation was becoming worse and worse. My mother's face came in front of eyes, "I had to face this situation."

I stood straight erect, motionless, speechless, looking to the front, full of anxiety and nervousness inside but showing strictness and courage on the outer side.

"Good Morning. What is your name?"

Ohh. I spoilt it. I even hadn't wished them. My tongue stuck out.

"Good morning sir and ma'am. I am Mrinal Ranjan Pathak."

"Okay, have a sit."

I was unable to look at their eyes, for I knew that I would be pissed off if I look at them. They gave me goosebumps.

I adjusted myself on the chair.

"Ok. Hand me over your documents."

I took out my folded certificates from the cloth bag. Someone laughed, I could hear. I ignored. I was feeling too insulted. I took a deep breathe again, moved by head up a bit, looked at the interviewer in front of me and handed him the certificates.

It was the first time in those 5-10 minutes that I had eye contact with someone.

"Have you brought your resume?"

I had forgotten the most important document for the interview. "No sir"

Another man to his left asked, "Did you really come for the interview?"

I knew there was no matter lying to them. It was better to say the truth and be shooed away rather than proving my stupidity by lying to them.

"Sir, I was unaware of this interview. I just read for the vacancy and came here."

The interviewer moved his lips up. It seems he disliked my answer.

"Ok fine. Describe yourself and your family member."

Questions were thrown, first personal, then technical and then some insulting.

"Do you know to use computer?"

"Yes sir, my typing speed in college was 100 wpm..."

"What is it now?"

"Sir, I don't have computer now."

"Okay. Ms. Anshu, would you like to ask something?"

My head turned down.

"Do you consider yourself eligible for this post? Why should we hire you?"

*****

Yes, it was a fact. Why should they hire me? There were so many smart candidates. Was I really eligible? But I had to say something to prove myself – that I was not dumb.

"Your organisation seems to a big one and I hope that in big organizations, the successful people work hard. The cook of a big restaurant bears up all the heat in preparing delicious foods for customers and he seldom has any time to look at his dressing or outfit. Similarly, while your company reaches new height, I will do my hard work in the backend.

My patience is very high, which is basic requirement for IT programmers. I paddled my bicycle 35 kilometers before reaching here, then waited till the lunch break was over and then stood in a queue under the scorching sun ray; but then too, I am sitting here with a cool mind. That shows the difference between me and other people. These are some reasons for hiring me. I assure you that you won't regret by hiring me to the post."

A crooked interviewer interrupted, "Okay we will look into it. We have many more candidates. You may leave now."

My chances were over. I stood to leave.

"Wait for the results. They will be out in an hour.", said Anshu.

The way the interviewers treated me- especially Anshu and that crooked man, I was quite assured that there was no meaning of staying. I was about to leave, but then I remembered that I had left the original documents inside. I rushed towards the door, knocked it a few times. But no one opened.

The security at the entry gate shouted at me, "Hey Mister, The gate will open only when the results will be out. Go and sit quietly."

There were lot of candidates waiting for the results. I was too waiting – not for the results but for my certificates that had no ability to define my results.

*****☒

The crowd rushed towards the board like the buzz of bees. The gate was open and I made my way through the crowd, pushing and pulling others.

I was deep into my thoughts, my time was all wasted.

"I couldn't find any day time job, how would I get all that money for my mother's operation."

Pushing and pulling everyone, I made my way towards the open door. I had to reach there by 10 PM. I didn't want my money to be deducted.

Finally, I left the crowd backwards. I heard some sounds, "Mrinal? Who is this Mrinal?"

I turned backwards but…. May be I was mistaken. The crowd was disappearing slowly.

I knocked the door. The interviewers were seating there around a round table enjoying their tiffin. They pointed me to come in.

"Congratulations for your new jouney.", one of the interviewer said.

I couldn't understand what was it. I thought into my mind, "Why are they congratulating me?"

"Sorry Sir, may be you are having some misunderstanding. I am here to take my certifiates, which I left during the interview."

They all laughed aloud. Anshu looked very beautiful while she smiled.

Suddenly turning towards me, she asked, "Did you see the result?"

"No". What was there in seeing the result when one knows that the he had his worst interview with the panel.

The other interviewer gave a smirk smile and said, "Mrinal you have been selected for the post. Here, take your joinig letter."

I couldn't believe myself. It was a moment my mind had got blanked and it was confused to understand or read anything. And then the words in the joining letter, 'Salary- Basic Pay of Rs. 25,000….. Facilities- Home accomodation, Vehicle conveyance, and whole lots of allowances added to it….' I just looked at the interviewers. My body stayed motionless like a statue that had been frozen by ice.

It took me some time to digest the news. "Thank You Sir. I was unaware of this result."

The peon brought my tiffin and asked me to sit. I looked at my sweaty and dirty dresses. But, then the plate of samosa, chutni and aloo chops; who could betray these. I just sat on the chair and myself comfortable.

While they instructed me all about the rules, regulations and codes of the organization, I only listened to them and enjoyed my tiffin.

"Okay Mrinal, you enjoy the meal. We have some small work left in the office. Remember to reach here by 9 AM sharp. You will get your uniform and then we will have some formalities."

"Okay sir sure."

They all turned back to go. Anshu too got up. She picked up her plate to leave.

"Thank you, Anshu. You have given me the job and you don't know how much you helped me. Thank a lot."

She turned back, gave a serious look, turned back to see if the interviewers had gone and seeing them waiting for her, she said with her teeth closed in a soft rude tone, "Let me remind you

Mrinal, I am not Anshu. My name is Ms. Anshudhara Chingole. And I am your senior, never forget that. You are my worst enemy.”

Listening to these my ears hurt a bit. I just looked at the way which she talked to me. She had changed completely. Could years of separation have such a bad impact?

“Sorry, Ms. Anshudharaa. But I had one more question. If I am your worst enemy then why did you give me this job?”

She smiled. And looking her smile, my face too glowed up. But it did not last long.

“I like my enemies to be near me, so that I could look them crying, I could torture them. And see, you are my junior, I am your superior; You know how nice it would be to hear ‘Maam, Ma’am’ from your mouth. You would request me for leave and no matter what, I would have the complete freedom to scold you, insult you and making a bigger issue of nothing. And then, I would just kill your career While this company will give you money, it will load you with hell lots of obligations, burden, agreements and a conduct certificate, that you may never use to show your conduct wherever you go."

Her words echoed. She smiled, turned back and went away.

The samosas didn't taste the way it tasted before.

"My life was just a hell and will always will be hell". Having taken all the certificates in my bag, I was ready for the night job.

*****

Would Anshu Welcome Me?

I was woken by the barking dogs. I searched my pocket, and thanked god, my first income from the night duty was safely there in my pocket. I just took out the money and hid it inside my trouser's inner pocket.

"Rs. 1320, not a bad income for a day. " I did overtime work and the fat man gave me extra money for it. He then deducted some money from it mentioning them as charges for food, daily uses and space to sleep, but then it didn't made me sad, because it was my first income.

My eyes were paining. It was only 4 hours of sleep. I had to do the breakfast.

Breaking a stick from the neem tree, I brushed myself and took a fresh bath with the cooled water that poured down from an overflow tank. Having finished all my work, I wore the best piece of cloth that I had in my bag, and then I was ready to set up my new jouney.

The guard welcomed me. He asked me for sweets. I smiled, held his hand and promised him to give him from my first month's salary. He just nodded.

As I entered the sliding door of the building, the peon greeted me and took me. The board read, "HRM Associate".

I was provided with my uniform. I was then out in a uniform, white full sleeved shirt, a dotted black tie, black belt, black trousers and shiny black shoes. I looked myself up in the mirror.

"Amazing. Young, handsome and such a corporate look. But something was missing. I combed my hair, dusted some powder on my face, and yes, now it was all perfect."

I was ready. Then I ws shown my locker, and then I was headed to the HRM section, where they provided me with ID cards, laptops and lots more of documents. The office was big, air conditioned and aromatic. The hanging lights and small plants on table tops and on the entrances added up to its beauty.

Hours passed by reading and signing all those documents. While I felt good about all these, but I couldn't forget what Anshu said. I was made aware of the organisation, various policies, leave system and everything that was left.

Finally, the manager rang the bell and another staff stepped inside. He guided me towards a project room. Anshu and her team sat their with their laptops.

Anshu called me inside. I marched slowly; my mind preoccupied with the lots of fear.

She introduced me up.

"Hello guys, May I have your attention here. He is Mr. Mrinal and has joined the office today. He will work with us. He is new here and hope you will all co-operate with him and help him."

Now started the real introduction.

"Since you all know that our project has been delayed, we need to do our best. And we want only experienced persons, so you will have to force him up to work. I need work from him by hook or by crook. If it is found that he is not working well, then he need not come to office, until his work is completed from home. And on this condition, the payroll section will not have any problem deducting his salary."

She pointed towards a chair. "Go sit there"

I went there, looking down. I felt very insulted. She had made a very bad impression of me in front of my colleagues in the first day itself.

*****

I tried to learn but none of them seemed to help me. They just gave me the task, without even making me understand the idea of the task.

As time passed by, Anshu came , insulted me infront of everyone and went away. Who did like to bear this insult? I never liked it.

You would think that why I didn't leave the job?

I felt; I felt to leave the job but I was dependent, I had a huge responsibility resting upon my shoulders. 'I *miss you Maa very much'*. Tears rolled down from my eyes; the place was inconvenient to cry. I got up, pushed my chair back and came out of the room. The door slammed behind me. Asking about the direction, I reached the toilet and released all my frustration after making sure that no one was inside.

There was no one to share my feelings except me. The heavy tear drops came out ; my mind and my body felt a bit lightened up.

I washed my face, closed my fist and said to myself looking in the mirror, "I can do it. Yes, I can bear up for the sake of my mother. I am coming home soon, Mom."

*****

The beginning three days went making fun of me, laughing and teasing me, but my calmness and patience made them change. Their comments had reduced to a great extent.

I tried to work with them, but Anshu always insulted me.

"He cannot work. It is not planting trees or harvesting. It is programming, and it needs focus, attention and a stable mind. See this creature. Do you think he can help us?"

That was my chain to which I was bound, for I couldn't leave the job or complain any one about my situation.

As the international conference approached, they started doing their work.. They failed. I saw them losing and I too belt bad when they all sat with their heads resting upon their hands; I wanted to help, but I was helpless, for I had almost eaten up the programming that I learnt.

There was also a fear in my mind, lest I lose, they will again make fun of me. So, I sat their looking at Anshu than at her colleagues. It was true, that they used to alleviate their frustration by scolding me and insulting me.

The next two days were totally unrest. From the morning till the evening, my sounds could hear only the 'tiktak kadak' sound of the key board.

The clock read 5 PM.

"We have failed. I don't think we can do anything more", one of Anshu's colleagues said with grief.

Anshu looked at me and shouted releasing all her frustration, "This is due to this person. Are you taking money to sit idle? You made us lose our focus. Get outtttttttt!!!!"

These words from her… I couldn't bear more… I just left the spot leaving them alone.

I wasn't feeling well – both mentally and physically. I was not in a state to do my night duty; but I had to do it for my mother.

 As I cycled through the ups and down on the muddy road during the night duty, Anshu's harsh treatment made me sob.

Having completed the delivery, I headed towards the college. Narrating the entire story to the security guard, I went towards the library which was kept locked for most of the time. The guard unlocked the room and then gave me the keys.

The security guard was a nice man. He understood my pain and helped me during this time.

The whole day, I copied the files from the server, opened it, pasted it, ran the program, and every time the same message window popped up. "Errors Generated during Run Time".

My eyes had lost the sleep. I tried to grab up everything that I had forgotten in these years of gap. The guard made all arrangements for my food and checked that no one disturbed me.

The watch read, "3 AM…. 7:50AM….. 10:08AM….. 2:56 PM….. 5:30PM….."

The sun had already set. The security guard knocked at the door to close the room.

"Please give me some time. I just need some moments to have the job done."

The security went away. I looked at my watch. It was 6:30 PM. I opened the glass window. My eyes were itching probably due to little rest and my mind was quite disturbed by the continuous failure. The thought of my failure and my insult made me feel guilty.

The fresh air rushed through the glass window and touched my face. A new life embraced me.

Taking a deep breathe, I started again. Everything was silent except the knocking sound of the keyboard. Time went by. The security came after every few minutes, saw me and then went hanging his head down.

Hours flew like seconds. Finally, the last thrust on the ENTER key.

...INITIALIZING....ASSEMBLING PACKAGES....COMPILING.....

I joined both hands. Warm wind blew from my nose. Even the cold air conditioner and the breeze from the window couldn't stop my sweating. I just prayed God.

"YESSSSSSSSSSSSSSSSSSSSSSSSSSSSSSSSSSSSSSSSSSSSS! I did it". The screen showed "SUCCESS"

The security came up running hearing me scream. I just said him sorry for the delay and rushed as fast as I could. There was only 20 minutes left for my night job.

Down the stairs, through the sliding gate and then towards the main door; unlocked my bicycle and paddled it. The pedal slipped and 'OH GOD!!!!!', the chain came out from the sprocket.

Having loaded my cycle and myself on a auto rickshaw, I reached there at exact 10 PM.

*****

Two days of 4 hours sleep and continuous work on computer had made my eyes swollen. Reaching the office, I directly took a back seat and then the incidents thereafter were unknown to me.

*****

"Ahhh", I woke up startled. Someone pinched me.

The girls group laughed like the demons as if laughing for the first time in these 10 years.

"You know that we have failed in our project. Don't you feel shame? You are sleeping happily here? Who will go and report the boss about this? I don't even understand how this project failed. It never happened since I joined here, but this is the first time..."

Her tone changed from rudeness to soft; so soft that the words than turned broken.

"I...promotion...project....manager....international ...first...time...project...failed.....I....fired"

It was for the first time that I saw tears in her eyes. Before my mind could respond to this situation, the office gate opened, the boss entered. He was new to me, a long sturdy man with perfectly trimmed beard. He looked very decent and generous, but his appearance didn't match his attitude.

"Where is the project? Don't you know that within 15 minutes there will be international conference? I want the project to be submitted to me now. I want to go through it", the boss screamed.

"Sir, actually....", Anshu looked towards the ground as she said softly, "Actually.... The project...."

"Sir, actually the project has been completed since 1 day, but we are testing the application to check if any runtime errors are coming in different versions."

All eyes turned towards me. I became the centre of attention. The audience's mouth were wide open. Anshu couldn't understand anything, she just looked as I continued my talk with the boss.

"Very Good. Errors come during testing and it is very good idea to test the application several times before launching it to the market. But..", the Boss scratched his beard, "I didn't recognise you. Who are you?"

"Sir, I am the new assistant programmer. Anshu…", my tongue stuck out, "Sorry, Ms. Anshudhara Chingole guided us and inspired the team throughout the journey, which made us complete this large project within the stipulated time."

Anshu looked at me with surprise, but I knew that in case the project had been incomplete, Anshu would have to bear up all the things..

"Very Good Ms. Anshudhara. You deserve this position."

"Thank You sir. ", she smiled, but not from her heart. The boss went away.

As the boss moved out. The team completely burst upon me. Anshu came to the front and yelled, "Why did you lie? Now what will we do? We haven't even completed the project and you say that it is under testing mode…." Questions went by as I listened to them. Finally, her chattering mouth stopped by the last statement, "Are you dumb?"

"Anshu…", She gave me a look with her big eyes popping out. "Sorry, Anshudhara Ma'am, please turn on the projector."

One of Anshu's colleagues switched the projector on. After few seconds of reloading, the white screen displayed – "APPLICATION TESTED SUCCESSFULLY. NO CRASHES FOUND."

Anshu couldn't believe, she took the mouse and began checking the dashboard. She clicked on all the tabs that she could, and after verifying it, she jumped and clapped with happiness.

"Wow, amazing. How did you do this?"

I just smiled and said nothing. She gave me a flirty look and scurried towards the boss office. In the mean while her colleagues started talking and flirting. That day was a turning point in my life. Few minutes later Anshu came out and said to all her colleagues, "Boss says that we need to go to Auditorium to practice for the application launch event…"

As she talked with her colleagues, I kept changing my position from her left to the front and then to the right to grab her attention but she kept turning her head to the opposite direction of my movement. She ignored me.

The team took the stroll towards the auditorium. I followed them.

Anshu being the leader discussed the plan.

"The program would start with lighting the candle and then an introduction tune. This will be followed by a brief discussion of the company's journey by the boss. Then the anchors would call me, and I will describe about the project; after that I will call the members and you all will come one by one from the left side of the stage. Okay?"

Everyone shouted at once, "Okay Ma'am"

"So, shall we start?"

"Yes ma'am, sure", one of the colleagues said.

Anshu got up in the stage, she did her role well. Perhaps she had been preparing since long for this day. The speech went as I prepared myself for entry.

The names went by, "And the team members are- Mehak Kumari , Project Finalizer... Anamika Dubey, Senior Programmer... ", the names went by, as I waited for the entry, "And finally, the last but not the least, Mr. Prabin Choudhary, the Boss, our Director, who gave us this oppurtinity to prove our talent in this International Conference."

I stood waiting.. but my name wasn't taken. Though I could hear her colleagues "What about Mrinal? Why didn't you call her... You know very well that this project was only successful due to his efforts....", but there was no reply from her. They crossed me, while I stood overcoming my emotions and staring at Anshu.

*****

The days had seemed. It was a bit well because these days Anshu's colleagues and my co-workers didn't laugh at me. They smiled at me, but neither of them talked with me.

Practice sessions went by, and I always kept standing on the left side of the stage, waiting for my name to come. But that day never came.

My body felt a bit unstable. A week of incomplete sleep had made my body too tired, and the insult along with mistreatment in the office had made me mentally unstable to join the office.

But there was much work left for the day. I had to ask for leave from the director to allow me to go to my village and deposit the advance in the City Hospital for my mother's operation. There was nothing much left in the office and the International Conference. All I got from my hard work was insult, ignorance and mental irritation. There was nothing more that I could do.

Keeping all the pain aside, I counted the money left with me, it was Rs.10,347

I wrapped those Rs.100 notes and then tied them with a thread, keeping Rs.47 with me for my expenses. Keeping the bundle deep inside the cloth bag, I took myself off towards the office.

****

 Depositing the bag in the counter, I whispered to the security, "Please keep this bag with safety. I have some valuables inside it."

The security was well aware with my family's situation and my only reason to work here. He smiled, "Babu, you go and do not take tension. I will take care."

I smiled back, "Thank You"

Little rain drops sparkled as it fell on the marble tiles. This was an unseasonal rainfall. I was in hurry; I had to deposit the money as soon as possible. I chose to take the shortcut path, keeping my feet very securely upon the tiles for a firm grip. These formal shoes were very slippery on this tiled floor.

From nowhere, Anshu appeared before me and seeing me so close to her, she stopped herself with a sudden jerk; but lost her balance and fell into my arms.

'Her dark eyes met with me and the curve of her eyebrows on her fair forehead gave a perfect beauty. The rose red lips and the glossy look and her smooth curly hairs added to her cuteness. I was lost in her.'

As I lifted my hand to touch her face, she lurch me down.

My heartbeat increased and my eyes could see the approaching marble tiles.

"Dhoooommmmmm!", I fell down with my face down.

*****

My eyes couldn't believe the situation when my eyes opened. My parents were standing in front of me, and my mother was perfectly well. I tried lifting my neck, but my nose pained. It took me a bit to realise that my nose was not in a good condition.

Before I could ask anything, my mother rushed towards me and sat beside me. With tears in her eyes she asked, "Are you fine Beta? I am seeing you after such a long time, why did you leave the home?"

"Maa I came to earn money for your operation."

"Ohh!!! MY lovely Beta", saying this she kissed my hands.

"Maa, how are you? And what about the operation?"

My father coming in front said, "Those doctors are really fools. They will someday kill the living one by misplacing their reports. It's we who suffer. Thanks to the security of your company who called us. We were fed up searching for you..."

Agreeing with my father, my mother added, "And also thanks to Anshu beta, she has been helping us. It was good that she sent a car to receive us."

"Mom you don't know her, she is very selfish. It is due to her that I am here."

"No beta, it was just a co-incidence. She is a very good girl. Throughout the journey she kept saying sorry, and also narrated to us the whole story of how rude she has been to you."

"Maa, you don't know anything. She is just saying these because she doesn't want a police case upon her."

"Beta, if this had been the case then she would have gone away when the doctor said that you are fine, the previous day. But she waited for you and has just left somewhere few hours ago."

I couldn't believe my ears. Why did Anshu did all these? Why?

"Beta, " my father said, "it was you who did the mistake. You should never use a girl."

"But Papa, I didn't use her either."

"But, you just broke her heart. A girl can understand everything even though you make excuses. Remember, dear boy, we know that we are poor, and our caste is low. And that is not under our control. If you had rejected her for only these reasons, it might not had hurt her so much, but because she doesn't look and has a dark color doesn't mean that she is not fit to become a life partner. Love should happen by heart and not by color, caste or outward appearance."

"Papa, I am sorry. I didn't know she would be so beautiful in these few years."

"See, this is your mistake. Today also you judge her by her outer beauty. If you want to love someone, love her inner beauty and not just her outer beauty, because the outer beauty remains only with age, but it is the inner beauty that keeps your mother and me together in a tied and happy relationship."

"Papa, I love her smile. Papa I am feeling too bad."

I started crying. My parents wiped off my tears, "Beta she said she will come after some time. Tell her sorry. If she hadn't been there, we don't know if we could even see you."

My mom was right. May be I had hurt her very badly. I knew that I had rejected her due to my parent's happiness, but now it seemed that my parents would be much happier to accept her; and I had long wished for this day.

*****

The door opened, she came in running, directly through the door and after taking a sharp turn, came and held my hands and gave me a light hug.

"I am Sorry", and started crying.

With my other hand, I stroke her hairs. Her eyes looked red, swollen and enveloped with tears.

"I really didn't knew that your family situation had been so worse.. and I mistreated you...", saying these she burst into tears.

I held her head with both my hands and kissed on her forehead. "I am too sorry", I pulled her upon and hugged her tightly. My parents watched me as the tears of sadness rolled down their eyes.

She realized that my parents are looking at us, and got up.

"I have brought something for you Mrinal."

"What? Insults?", I said as I cracked into laughter.

"No, Eat this...", opening a tiffin, unfolding the piece of food, she brought her hand forward. And the first bite of the food reminded me of something.

"Achar Dosaaaaaaaaa? Wow, where did you get it? It is tastier than it used to be."

She smirked and said, "I made it. I had learnt it after we were separated."

Now, I pulled her, and hugged her again more tightly. She wrapped her hands towards me and the kisses landed. My maa and papa looked at each other and moved out, leaving us alone.

The time had stopped and she was in my arms... Kissing me and loving me.. But this broken nose of mine disturbed this moment...

"Oh God!, Why this happens to me? I got what I wanted, but then I can't even kiss her properly... Oh my nose hurts...."

The story that started with Achar Dosa ended with Achar Dosa.. But there was difference-difference in the feelings that we had towards each other.

*****

The International Conference was postponed due to rain and was rescheduled one month later. This time Anshu called all the team members, then the Boss. Mrinal was then too surprised as to why she didn't call him, although everything was fine?

Finally he was about to leave from the backdoor of the stage, but then the announcement went- "And last but not the least, the most awaited member of the organisation who gave everything for this project, his dedication, his hard work and patience, by which we have reached this height; I want to call on the stage, Mr. Mrinal Ranjan Pathak."

Oh my God. Was I to be happy or should I cry?

"I walked towards the centre, the spot light followed me. The whole crowd stood up and clapped for me." Looking the complete audience cheer at me, the heartbeat synchronized with the clapping sound. The camera's flashed when the complete team lifted the award. While everybody's eyes were upon the trophy, my eyes were deep drowned into her and her eyes drowned into me.

*****

Epilogue

Mrinal took the last sip of the drinks as he said all these. He got up, smiled back... Looked at the watch and said , "Finally, my story is now completed. Hope I didn't bore you or waste your time."

"No Mrinal, it was super exciting to know that your love story was successful. I just want to thank you from the core of my heart for completing your long-waited incomplete story." I got up from the chair and tapped on his shoulders. "I need to go Mrinal. " I gave him a smile and left.

As I was flying on my economy class, I remembered that Mrinal's story had gathered a lot of crowd in the train where he narrated. But, none of them could hear the complete story.

Today as I sit idle, I brought this whole story into pen and paper, for I had to let all those people know about this happy conclusion.

*****

www.ingramcontent.com/pod-product-compliance
Lightning Source LLC
Chambersburg PA
CBHW051248150726
48001CB00019B/1661